Kent, Jack, 1920-1985
Mrs. Mooley/written and illustrated by Jack Kent.
p. cm.
Summary: Inspired by a picture in the nursery rhyme book left on the barn floor, Mrs. Mooley, the cow, is determined to jump over the moon, despite the ridicule of the other barnyard animals.
$12.95
[1. Cows--Fiction. 2. Domestic animals--Fiction. 3. Perseverance (ethics)--Fiction.] I. Title.
[PZ7.K414Mr 1993]
[E]--dc20   92-47064
                                                                CIP
                                                                AC

Mrs. Mooley

Written and illustrated by
Jack Kent

An Artists & Writers Guild Book
Golden Books
Western Publishing Company, Inc.
850 Third Avenue, New York, New York 10022

There was something on the floor of the barn. Mrs. Mooley went over to see what it was.

"Why," she said, "it's the book the farmer's little boy was reading. He must have dropped it."

Mrs. Mooley couldn't read, but she enjoyed looking at the pictures.

There was a picture of three men in a tub.

There was a picture of an old woman who lived in a shoe.

There was a picture of a *cow jumping over the moon!*

"What fun!" cried Mrs. Mooley. She gave a little jump just for practice.

Mrs. Mooley came down with a jolt that shook the whole barn.

"Hey!" squawked the hen. "You're jostling my eggs!
What do you think you're doing?"

"I'm practicing," said Mrs. Mooley. "I'm going to
jump over the moon."

"Jump over the moon?" repeated the hen. *"Kut kut kahawww,"* she cackled.

She laughed so hard, she hatched two of her eggs.

The pigeon in the loft laughed at Mrs. Mooley.
The mouse in the straw laughed at Mrs. Mooley.
"What's so funny?" the goose wanted to know.
They could hardly stop giggling long enough to tell
her. Finally they gasped out the news.

"Honk haaaa kahonk! "
The goose laughed so hard,
she lost three tail feathers.

The goose told the duck.

"*Quaaaack!*" laughed the duck and told the horse.

The horse laughed so hard, he got the hiccups.
"What's going on?" asked the pig.

"Mrs. Mooley *hic!* says she's going to *hic!* jump over the *hic!* moon," the horse told the pig.

The pig laughed so hard, he flopped into a mud puddle, which was where he planned to be, anyway.

When he came up for air, he told the goat about Mrs. Mooley.

The goat laughed.
The pig laughed.
The horse laughed.
The duck laughed.
The goose laughed.
The mouse and the pigeon laughed.
The hen and her chicks laughed.

They all laughed at Mrs. Mooley until it was bedtime.

All of the animals went to sleep. All except Mrs. Mooley. She was out in the barnyard, jumping up and down.

"All it takes is determination," she said to herself, "and a little practice!"

All night long Mrs. Mooley jumped and jumped. And the moon shone down from high above her.

Mrs. Mooley was still jumping when a faint light in the eastern sky told that morning was coming.

The moon began to sink in the west. Its trip across the sky was ending.

The cock crowed, and one by one the animals woke up.
The moon was so low that it seemed to be sitting on the
ground. In a few minutes it would be gone. Mrs. Mooley had
time for one last jump.

It was her highest jump yet.

The animals saw the moon sitting on the ground.
They saw Mrs. Mooley jump high in the air. They saw
Mrs. Mooley *jump over the moon!*

"She DID it!" screeched the hen. She was so excited, she hatched another egg.

The goose was so excited, she lost another tail feather.

The horse was so excited, his hiccups came back.

And the pig flopped into the mud puddle again.

"You DID it, Mrs. Mooley!" they all shouted at once.
"You jumped over the moon!"

"All it takes is determination," said Mrs. Mooley, "and
a little practice."

"I think I'll jump over the sun next," Mrs. Mooley
went on. "No cow ever did that before."

"Jump over the SUN?" oinked the pig, and he fell back
into the mud puddle. But only because he wanted to.

Nobody laughed at Mrs. Mooley this time.

"And after I jump over the sun, who knows?" said Mrs. Mooley. "There are a lot of stars and planets to jump over."

"Do you really think you could?" asked the horse.

"Why not?" said Mrs. Mooley, and she gave a tired sigh as she lay down in the hay. "All it takes is determination and . . ."

Mrs. Mooley's eyes blinked shut.

She was fast asleep.

". . . and a little practice," said the hen, who didn't like
anything left unfinished.